Crumble
and Custard

and Other Puppy Tales

Crumble
and Custard
and Other Puppy Tales

Jenny Dale

Illustrated by Susan Hellard
and Frank Rodgers

A Working Partners Book

MACMILLAN CHILDREN'S BOOKS

'Gus the Greedy Puppy', 'Spot the Sporty Puppy' and 'Lily the Lost Puppy'
first published 1999, and 'Crumble and Custard' first published 2001,
in four separate volumes by Macmillan Children's Books

This bind-up edition published 2017 by Macmillan Children's Books
an imprint of Pan Macmillan
20 New Wharf Road, London N1 9RR
Associated companies throughout the world
www.panmacmillan.com

Created by Working Partners Limited
London WC2B 6XF

ISBN 978-1-5098-6046-3

Contents

Crumble and Custard

Special thanks to Narinder Dhami

Chapter One

"Is Oliver coming yet?" Crumble whined. The Labrador puppy was trying to climb up onto the sofa. He was using his brother Custard as a stepping stone.

"Get your paw out of my ear, Crumble!" Custard woofed crossly.

"Help me get onto the sofa, then,"

Crumble panted, trying to heave himself up. "I want to climb onto the window ledge and look for Oliver."

"What's going on here?" a voice barked suddenly.

Crumble was so surprised, he let go of the sofa and tumbled onto the floor. Luckily, Custard broke his fall.

"What *are* you doing?" yapped Lady the spaniel, padding into the room.

"I was trying to climb up onto the sofa to see if Oliver was coming," Crumble woofed.

"You *know* you're not allowed on the sofa," Lady replied sternly.

"You're a bad boy, Crumble!" Custard

barked, giving his brother a teasing nip on the tail. Next moment they were rolling around on the carpet, play-fighting.

"What are you two up to?" said Mrs James, popping her head round the door. Crumble and Custard belonged to Mrs James's son, Oliver. But while he was at work they stayed with Mrs James and her old spaniel, Lady.

"Nothing, Granny James!" Crumble and Custard barked together, putting on their best "cute" faces. Suddenly the ears of both puppies pricked up.

"I can hear a motorbike!" Crumble woofed excitedly.

"It's Oliver," Custard barked. "And I heard it first!"

"No, *I* did," Crumble yapped.

Still arguing, the two pups rushed to the front door.

A moment later, Oliver came in. Custard and Crumble went mad, jumping around his feet and barking loudly.

"Hello, boys!" said Oliver, grinning. He took off his crash helmet and ran a hand through his fair hair. Then he scooped the pups up, one in each arm. "Have you been good today?"

"*I* have," Crumble yapped, licking his owner's cheek. "But Custard ran off with Lady's biscuit!"

"Ooh, I did not!" Custard woofed back, nibbling Oliver's ear. "Anyway, Granny James told Crumble off for chewing the rug!"

"What have you been cooking today, Oliver?" Crumble pushed his nose into Oliver's neck. Their owner was a chef, so he always smelled *delicious*.

7

In fact, biscuit-coloured Crumble and pale yellow Custard were named after Oliver's favourite pudding.

The pups knew that Oliver went to people's houses to cook food for them when they were having special parties. Crumble and Custard always thought it was *most* unfair that they weren't allowed to go along too.

"Hi, Mum," Oliver said. "Thanks for looking after the Terrible Two."

"It's a pleasure – sort of," his mum laughed. "Now, you three, enjoy your weekend."

"We will," Oliver promised.

Crumble and Custard looked at each

other in delight. So tomorrow was the weekend! That meant Oliver wouldn't leave them and go to work. He'd stay at home and play!

"Brilliant!" the two pups barked, their tails wagging happily.

"Bye, Mum," Oliver called as he carried Crumble and Custard over to his motorbike. "You have a good weekend too, and give my love to Gran."

"Lady and I will be back from Gran's on Sunday night," his mum replied. "So I'll be here to look after the pups as usual on Monday morning."

Oliver's motorbike had a sidecar which Crumble and Custard could ride in. They loved it. The sidecar had a cover attached, which meant that they were quite safe. It was clear, so that they could look out too.

"OK, boys, let's go," Oliver said, popping the pups into the sidecar and closing it carefully.

"A whole weekend with Oliver," Crumble yapped happily as their owner revved up the motorbike engine.

"Fantastic!" Custard agreed.

At first, the weekend went just as Crumble and Custard had hoped.

On Saturday morning they all had a lie-in. The puppies curled up in their favourite place next to Oliver. Then they all went down to the kitchen. First, Oliver fed Crumble and Custard their puppy food, then he got out the pancake pan to make his own breakfast.

Crumble, who always finished eating first, snuffled around Oliver's feet as he began to mix the pancake batter. "Yum!" he yapped. "Leave a bit of room for some pancake, Custard!"

"Don't worry, I will!" Custard snuffled back, as he finished off his puppy biscuits.

Just then the phone rang. Oliver went into the hall to answer it. The puppies rushed after him.

"Go away!" Crumble barked crossly as Oliver picked up the phone. "Oliver's making pancakes."

"Yes, and you're not having any, whoever you are," Custard added.

"Quiet, boys," Oliver said sternly. "Hello?"

"Maybe we should guard the pancake mix," Custard growled. "Someone
might come and steal it."

"Good idea," Crumble agreed.

The two pups trotted back to the
kitchen.

"You're having an important lunch

party today, and you want me to come and cook for you?" Oliver was saying.

Crumble and Custard skidded to a halt outside the kitchen door when they heard *that*. Their tails stopped wagging. Oliver was going to *work* today? What about their lovely weekend?

"Well, I can see it's an emergency, Mrs Gill," Oliver said. "But I can't, I'm afraid."

The pups' tails began to wag again, just a little.

"I've got no one to look after my two puppies," Oliver went on. "They usually stay with my mum while I'm working, but she's away for the weekend. And I can't leave them on their own because they destroy things."

"That's because *you* chewed one of Oliver's wooden spoons, Crumble!" Custard yapped.

"Well, *you* ate half his rubber plant!" Crumble argued.

"I suppose I could . . ." Oliver was saying. "But only if there's somewhere safe for them to play while I'm working."

Crumble and Custard looked at each other. Did that mean what they thought it meant?

"OK," Oliver agreed, picking up a pen. "I'll bring the pups with me then. If you could just give me the address . . ."

"YES!" Crumble barked excitedly, running round in circles to celebrate. "Oliver's taking us with him."

"Yippee!" woofed Custard. "We're going with Oliver to cook party food. That's *much* better than going to the park!"

"Yes," Crumble agreed. "It's even better than a bit of pancake after breakfast!"

Chapter Two

"OK, boys, we're here." Oliver turned off the motorbike engine. "Look at this posh house!"

"It's huge!" Crumble gasped.

"Does the Queen live here?" asked Custard.

The Gills' house was at the end of a winding driveway. It had a large garden with a waterfall and lots of statues. Crumble and Custard could hardly wait to dive out of the sidecar and explore.

"Now listen, you two," Oliver said sternly. "I want you to be on your best behaviour. Is that clear?"

"Yes, Oliver," the pups woofed.

Oliver clipped their leads onto their collars, and let them out. He led them over to the front door. But before he had a chance to ring the bell, the door flew open.

A tall woman with black hair stood there, beaming at them. "Hello, I'm Mrs Gill," she said. "Thank goodness you could help me out, Oliver. And aren't your dogs gorgeous!"

Crumble and Custard liked Mrs Gill already. They snuffled at her fingers as she gave them both a quick pat.

"Come in," said Mrs Gill. She hurried them across a beautiful hallway with thick rugs and a sweeping staircase, then into a huge kitchen. "Like I told you on the phone, my usual chef has flu, and you can see what a mess we're in."

Crumble and Custard's eyes nearly popped out of their heads. They'd never *seen* so much food! There were containers and packets on all the worktops, as well as bags and boxes of colourful fruit and vegetables.

"*How* many guests did you say were coming to the party, Mrs Gill?" Oliver asked, looking just as dazed as the puppies.

"Oh, only twenty," Mrs Gill replied. "But my daughter Yasmin is having a birthday party in two days' time. That's why there's so much food." She waved a hand around the kitchen. "Use whatever you like. There's a joint of beef for the main course, but the starters and pudding are up to you."

"OK," Oliver agreed.

"The guests will be arriving at about two o'clock," Mrs Gill went on. "Come and see the dining room." She led them all out of the kitchen and into the big room next door.

It had a long wooden table that was laid with sparkling plates and cutlery, and huge bowls of flowers. Two large French windows stood open at the far end of the room, leading out into the garden.

Crumble and Custard both sniffed the air, their black noses twitching. There were loads of exciting new smells to explore!

A man wearing shorts and a T-shirt

hurried from the garden, into the room.

"This is my husband," said Mrs Gill. "Darling, say hello to Oliver, our new chef."

Smiling, Mr Gill came across the room. "Thanks for coming to our rescue like this," he began. Then he spotted Crumble and Custard, and stopped in his tracks. "Oh no! Keep those dogs away from me!"

"Don't worry," Oliver said quickly, "they're very friendly."

"Oh, no, it's not that," Mr Gill muttered. He began to sneeze loudly. "*A-tishoo!*"

"Oh, I forgot about your allergy!" said Mrs Gill. "You'd better go upstairs, darling."

Still sneezing, Mr Gill hurried over to the door, keeping as far away from the two puppies as he could.

"What's the matter with *him*?" Crumble asked. Mr Gill hadn't even given them a pat.

"Maybe he's got a cold," Custard suggested. "Remember when Oliver had one? He kept sneezing all the time."

"The puppies should be quite safe in the garden," Mrs Gill went on. "My daughter Yasmin's out there somewhere. She'll love them."

Oliver nodded. "I'll just get them settled, and then I'll start work."

"Super," said Mrs Gill. "Oh, excuse me." And she dashed off to answer the phone.

"Come on, Oliver," Crumble and Custard woofed together. They began to drag him towards the garden. "Let's go and explore."

Chapter Three

"*Please* let us off our leads, Oliver!" Crumble snuffled, as they walked through the enormous garden.

"Grr!" Custard grabbed his lead between his teeth and shook it crossly from side to side. "Let me go, Oliver!"

"Stop it, you two," Oliver scolded, unclipping their leads as they walked

26

across the lawn. "I just wanted to check that there's no way for you to get out of the garden."

"Look, Custard." Crumble had spotted something interesting.

"Where?" Custard woofed.

"There!" Crumble barked impatiently. "That must be Yasmin."

A girl with long black hair was lying on the grass ahead of them. She was reading a book.

Her eyes lit up at the sight of the two puppies. "Hi, I'm Yasmin," she called to Oliver. "Are you the chef?"

"Yeah, I'm Oliver, and this is Crumble and Custard," Oliver replied.

"I'm Crumble," Crumble panted. "Stroke me first!"

"I'm Custard," Custard yapped. "Stroke *me* first!"

Yasmin laughed. She bent down and put an arm round each puppy. "They're so cute," she cried. "Do you want me to look after them while you're working?"

"Oh, thanks!" Oliver said gratefully. "Sure you don't mind?"

Yasmin shook her head. "No, I love dogs."

"Great!" Crumble and Custard barked together.

"You two behave yourselves, then,"

Oliver said. He scratched the puppies' heads affectionately and handed their leads to Yasmin. "See you later."

"Look at me, Yasmin," Crumble woofed as Oliver hurried off. "I can roll over!" And he lay on the grass and rolled about, showing his fat tummy.

"No, look at me, Yasmin," Custard boasted. "I can catch my tail!" And he started running round in circles.

Yasmin grinned. "You're both lovely!" she said, kissing the tops of their heads.

Crumble and Custard had a brilliant time. They played Chase-the-Twig and Hide-and-Seek. And whenever the pups

got out of breath, Yasmin picked them up and gave them lots of cuddles.

"Let's go inside and have a drink," Yasmin suggested as they all lay panting on the grass after playing Tag. "And we can see how Oliver's getting on too."

As they got near the house, Crumble and Custard's noses began to twitch like mad. There were some *delicious* smells coming from the kitchen. They both began to feel very hungry as well as thirsty.

Oliver was spooning crumble over some apples in a large dish. His face was red because the kitchen was hot. But apart from that, he looked very calm and organised.

"I'm just going to get some water for the puppies, Oliver," Yasmin told him.

Oliver smiled at her. "Thanks," he said.

He grinned at Crumble and Custard. "Have you been good, boys?"

"*Course* we have," Crumble yapped proudly.

"Everything smells great, Oliver," Yasmin said shyly. She filled a bowl from the cold tap, then put it down on the floor. "How are you getting on?" she asked, as Crumble and Custard lapped at their water.

"Well, I've made the starters, and they're already in the dining room," Oliver said. "And I'm just finishing the pud. Then I'll put the beef in the oven. All I have to do then is chop the veggies and make salads."

"I can't wait to try it all," Yasmin grinned. Then she frowned as the sound of a car came through the open window. "I wonder who that is?"

"Well, as long as it's not the guests," Oliver laughed.

Yasmin went out into the hallway to have a look, and the puppies trotted after her.

"Wheeee!" Custard barked as he skidded on the polished floor. "This is fun, Crumble!"

Crumble tried to run after his brother, and slid along the floor too. "Let's see how far we can slide!" he yapped.

Yasmin stared out of the hall window.

A big car was pulling up outside the house, and another was just turning in through the gates. "Oh no!" she cried. "It *is* the guests – and it's only twelve o'clock! They're two hours early!"

Chapter Four

Crumble and Custard scrambled to a halt, mid-slide.

"The guests are here?" Crumble woofed. "They *can't* be."

"Go away," Custard growled. "Oliver's not ready yet."

Yasmin grabbed the pups and dashed back to the kitchen.

"Oliver!" she gasped. "The guests *are* here!"

"What?" Oliver was pouring custard into a jug. He was so surprised, he dripped some on the floor.

"Oh, yum," yapped Crumble and Custard, clambering out of Yasmin's arms to clean it up.

"See how helpful we are?" snuffled Crumble.

"What are we going to do?" Yasmin wailed. "Mum and Dad must have told them the wrong time."

Oliver looked at the large joint of beef. "Oh, no," he groaned. "The beef will never be ready in time. It will take hours to cook."

"Don't worry, Oliver," Crumble barked. "If we don't open the door, they'll all go away!"

"I'd better go and tell Mum and Dad," Yasmin said. She raced upstairs with the puppies at her heels. "Mum!" she yelled, running into her

37

parents' bedroom. "The guests are here!"

"What!" Mrs Gill rushed out of the bathroom. She was wearing her dressing gown, and she had a creamy facepack all over her face.

"Help!" Crumble barked. "Mrs Gill's face has turned green!"

"I'm scared," Custard whined, and tried to crawl under the bed.

"I don't believe it," Mrs Gill cried. "Will Oliver be able to serve lunch early?"

Yasmin shook her head. "He said that the beef isn't even in yet, and it will take hours to cook."

Just then the doorbell rang. Mrs Gill groaned.

"Who's that at the door?" Mr Gill came into the bedroom.

"It's the guests, Dad," Yasmin said urgently. "They're early."

"What?" Her dad glanced down at his shorts and T-shirt. "But I'm not even dressed yet – *a-tishoo*! Will somebody please take those dogs downstairs!"

"Show the guests into the sitting room, Yasmin," Mrs Gill said. She wiped her face with a tissue. "Offer them drinks and tell them we'll be down as soon as we can. Then tell Oliver to put the beef in the freezer and use the chicken drumsticks out of the fridge. They'll cook much more quickly. We can buy some more tomorrow for your birthday party."

Yasmin nodded and dashed downstairs again with the puppies right behind her.

"Mum and Dad are getting changed," she told Oliver breathlessly. "I've got to let the guests in and give them drinks. Oh – and forget the beef – do chicken drumsticks instead – they're in the fridge!" she called.

The doorbell rang again.

"OK, leave the pups here with me,"

said Oliver. He was looking *very* red in the face now.

Yasmin rushed out, shutting the kitchen door behind her.

Crumble and Custard crept quietly under the kitchen table, and sat cuddled close together.

"Poor Oliver," Crumble whined. "Will he get into trouble?"

"I don't know," Custard whimpered.

After a while, Yasmin came back. "Can I do anything to help, Oliver?" she asked.

Oliver nodded gratefully. "Put my crumble and custard in the dining room out of the way, will you?" Then he went into the pantry to fetch some potatoes.

"OK," Yasmin said. She picked up the pups and took them out of the kitchen.

"Don't *want* to go in the dining room," Crumble yapped.

"We want to stay with you," Custard snuffled.

"Now be good," Yasmin warned them as she put them in the dining room. And she shut the door quickly.

Crumble and Custard looked glum. But then, at exactly the same moment, their noses began to twitch.

"I smell food!" Crumble woofed excitedly.

"And it's close by!" Custard added.

Both pups bounded over to the big table, tails wagging.

"It must be up there!" Custard yapped. "Perhaps it's our lunch. That's why Oliver told Yasmin to put us in here."

"But how are we going to reach it?" Crumble woofed.

"Easy!" Custard yapped back. He began to climb up the nearest chair, using the bar to help him. It was a bit of a struggle, but he made it onto the seat. From there, he could just about get onto the top of the table.

"Hey, wait for me!" Crumble barked.

Custard was already sniffing at a long fish, covered with thin green things. He took a big bite as Crumble climbed up onto the table.

"Yum – and yuck!" Custard

spluttered. "The fish is nice, but that green stuff's horrible!"

"That's cucumber," Crumble said, taking a big bite himself. "Oliver puts it in sandwiches sometimes."

Custard turned to the other big plate. There was a big square of something meaty on it. "Mmm, this smells good!" he yapped. He took a lick. "Yes, it really *is* yummy!" he snuffled. This time he took a big bite.

Crumble, who had eaten half the fish by now, trotted over to have a taste, leaving muddy pawprints on the white tablecloth. "Oh, that's great!" he woofed when he tasted the meaty stuff.

45

His tail wagged so hard, he knocked a basket of toast triangles off the table.

Custard went over to a bowl of thick green liquid, licking the butter dish on the way. "Look at this," he woofed. "What do you think it is?"

"It looks like the cream Mrs Gill had on her face!" Crumble yapped back.

Custard wasn't so keen on tasting it after that. So he ate one of the crispy things next to it instead. "Help!" he barked. "It's hot!" He wiped his mouth on the tablecloth, trying to get rid of the taste.

*

Meanwhile, Yasmin was helping Oliver in the kitchen. She was washing lettuce whilst Oliver put the chicken drumsticks in the oven.

"Crumble and Custard are great," she sighed. "I wish I could have a puppy for my birthday. But I can't because of Dad's allergy."

"It's a shame," Oliver agreed. "I love Crumble and Custard to bits, even though they're naughty!"

He went over to the other end of the kitchen to get a saucepan. Then he stopped and stared at the big dish of crumble and jug of custard on the table.

"Yasmin," he said, puzzled, "I thought

you put my crumble and custard in the dining room?"

"I *did*—" Yasmin began. Then her face fell. "Oh NO!"

Chapter Five

"I thought you meant the puppies!" Yasmin groaned.

She and Oliver rushed out of the kitchen. "I didn't know you meant the *pudding*!"

"I was so busy, I didn't even notice the pups had gone!" Oliver muttered. "Let's hope they haven't done *too*

much damage . . ."

He opened the dining room door.

It was even worse than Oliver could have imagined. All the food was ruined. There were pawprints all over the tablecloth, and food had spilled on the floor. Crumble was just finishing off the fish. He had one cucumber slice stuck to his nose, and another on top of his head. Custard had decided to try the green stuff after all. His face was covered in it, just like Mrs Gill's facepack.

"My salmon! My pâté! My avocado dip and tortilla chips!" Oliver groaned.

"Hello," Crumble and Custard barked

brightly. "We're just finishing our lunch . . ." But their barks died away when they saw the look on Oliver's face.

"You bad, bad boys!" Oliver said. He sounded *very* stern. "Look what you've done!"

Crumble and Custard's ears flattened against their heads. They crept into the middle of the table and huddled there together, trying to make themselves as small as possible. They hated it when Oliver got angry.

"You've really done it now." Oliver was so cross, he could hardly speak. "*Look* at all this mess!"

"What's going on?" Mrs Gill appeared

in the doorway, wearing a smart black dress. She gasped as she stared round at the room.

Crumble and Custard whimpered unhappily, and tried to hide behind each other.

"It was my fault, Mum," Yasmin said quickly. "I put the puppies in here."

Mrs Gill looked at Crumble with his cucumber slices and Custard all covered in avocado dip. Then to everyone's relief, she smiled. "Nothing's going right today," she laughed.

Then Yasmin had an idea. "Hey! We could get Oliver to cook the rest of my party food," she said. "I don't mind.

We can always buy more tomorrow. And we've still got Oliver's lovely pudding!"

"Oh, why not?" said Mrs Gill. "And I'll take our guests into the garden – we won't be able to eat in here." She hurried out again.

Oliver glared at Crumble and Custard. "That's the last time you ever come to work with me," he snapped. Then he rushed back to the kitchen.

Yasmin picked up a napkin and wiped the puppies' faces.

"We're sorry, Yasmin," they whimpered sadly.

Yasmin gave them a hug. "Never

54

mind," she whispered. "Come on, let's help Oliver."

Oliver was rushing round the kitchen pulling things out of the fridge and the cupboards. "Chicken drumsticks, mini pizzas, hot dogs, crisps, sausage rolls, burgers," he muttered. "I don't think any of the guests will be expecting food like this!"

"Mmm, I like burgers," Crumble growled to Custard.

"I think we've had enough to eat," yapped Custard.

They both sat quietly under the kitchen table.

Mrs Gill opened the kitchen door. "Everyone's asking when lunch is going to be ready," she said.

"In about half an hour," Oliver said, putting a tray of mini pizzas in the oven. "Can you keep the guests happy until then?"

"Oh, I think so," said Mrs Gill, spotting the crisps and cheesy puffs that Yasmin had tipped into big bowls. "Come and pass those around, Yasmin," she said.

Then Mrs Gill spotted Crumble and Custard under the table. She smiled. "Come on, you two," she said, scooping them up. "You're going to entertain our guests until lunch is ready!"

"Er . . . that might not be such a good idea . . ." Oliver began.

"Yes, it is," Mrs Gill said firmly. "They're so cute, they'll take everyone's mind off their rumbling tummies!"

Oliver looked sternly at Crumble and Custard. "Well, you two just behave yourselves from now on," he warned them.

"We will," the two pups barked as they went out into the garden with Mrs Gill and Yasmin.

The garden seemed to be full of people.

Mr Gill was running around

arranging chairs and tables so that everyone could sit down.

"We thought we'd eat out here as it's such a nice day," he was saying brightly.

"I'm really looking forward to lunch," said a posh woman, who was wearing lots of gold jewellery.

"We will be eating in about half an hour," Mrs Gill announced calmly as she crossed the lawn, a puppy under each arm.

"Oh, I say, how cute!" exclaimed another woman, staring at Crumble and Custard. "They're not yours, are they?"

"No – *a-tishoo*!" said Mr Gill.

"They belong to our chef," Mrs Gill said. She put Crumble and Custard down on the grass.

The two pups really cheered up as everyone started ooh-ing and aah-ing, and saying how gorgeous they were.

"But I'm more gorgeous than *you*!" Crumble bit his brother's ear playfully.

"Ooh, no, you're not!" Custard protested, and attacked him.

They rolled over and over on the grass, pretending to fight. And then they ran round in circles trying to catch their tails until they were dizzy. Everyone

laughed and applauded, except for Mr
Gill, who was too busy sneezing.

Half an hour later, when Oliver
carried out trays of mini pizzas and
burgers, he could hardly believe his
eyes.

A well-dressed woman and two men
in *very* smart suits were on their hands

and knees on the grass playing with Crumble and Custard. Everyone else was watching and laughing.

"Crumble and Custard are a big hit," Yasmin said as she hurried to meet Oliver. "No one's mentioned food at all!"

Oliver smiled. "Maybe we'll get away with it," he said.

Crumble and Custard wagged their tails. Their owner wasn't angry any more.

"Well, here goes," said Mrs Gill. She took a tray of burgers from Oliver. "The guests are going to get a bit of a shock when they see what's on the menu!"

Crumble and Custard watched as Mrs Gill and Oliver carried the trays of food over to the guests. Would they like the food – or not?

Chapter Six

"That's the best lunch I've been to in ages!"

"Super idea to have kids' party food, wasn't it?"

"Yes, enormous fun!"

"And the pudding was wonderful – best crumble and custard I've *ever* tasted!"

Mrs Gill closed the front door behind the last guest, and smiled. "*Well!*" she said. "It seems our lunch was a big success!"

"Good," Crumble barked with a yawn. He snuggled down in Oliver's arms.

"Great," Custard added sleepily, as he did the same in Yasmin's.

"*A-tishoo!*" sneezed Mr Gill. "And we've got that huge joint of beef in the freezer."

"*And* we'll have to buy some more food for my party," Yasmin grinned.

"Yes, I had to go and cook more mini pizzas, burgers, *and* hot dogs," Oliver said. "There are none at all left now. I don't think the guests had eaten food like that for ages!" He glanced at his watch. "I think it's time we were going . . ."

Oliver carried Crumble and Custard outside and tucked them snugly into the sidecar.

Yasmin leaned inside and gave each puppy one last kiss. "Goodbye," she whispered. "I really wish I could have a puppy like you."

"Bye, Yasmin," the pups yapped sadly, as Oliver drove them away. "We're going to miss you . . ."

*

"And then all the guests said we were really cute, and started playing with us," Crumble barked.

"And they forgot all about the food," Custard added.

It was Monday afternoon, and the puppies were at Granny James's house. It was a sunny day, and they were out in the back garden with Lady.

"Did we tell you about Yasmin?" Crumble went on.

"She's our *best* friend," Custard woofed. "Except for Oliver, of course!"

The old spaniel yawned. "You've told me all this already. You've been going on about it all day!" And she padded off to have a snooze under the lilac tree.

"Do you think we'll ever see Yasmin again?" Crumble asked, as he and Custard ran around the garden chasing butterflies.

"I don't know." Custard snapped at a big, buzzing bee that flew right past his nose. "I hope so."

Just then Mrs James came to the back door. "Crumble! Custard!" she called. "I've got a surprise for you!"

"Oh, what?" Crumble barked, rushing towards her.

"I love surprises," panted Custard, who was right behind him.

"Is it a juicy bone?" Crumble woofed eagerly.

"Is it pancakes?" Custard asked.

But it wasn't either of those things.

"It's YASMIN!" Crumble and Custard barked loudly. They could hardly believe their eyes.

Yasmin was in the sitting room with Granny James. She rushed straight over to the puppies, and picked them both up.

"What are *you* doing here?" the puppies yapped happily, covering her face with kisses.

"My school's just round the corner from here," Yasmin said breathlessly.

"Oliver says I can come and visit you whenever I like, and Mum says it's OK too!"

"Oh, that's brilliant!" Crumble barked, thrilled to bits. "That's even better than a juicy bone!"

"And it's even better than pancakes!" Custard agreed joyfully.

Gus
the Greedy Puppy

To Beulah, who was the bravest of puppies

Chapter One

"Gus! Stop that!"

Gus didn't stop. He was enjoying himself. He'd found one of Mr Carter's ties lying on the bedroom floor and he was chewing it to bits.

"Gus!" Holly shouted again as she ran up the stairs towards him. "Give me that!"

No way! Gus thought. He hung on to one end of the tattered tie as Holly grabbed the other, and they both began to pull.

"Let go, Gus!" Holly squealed. "Dad's going to be mad when he sees what you've done!"

Gus couldn't understand why. After all, Holly's dad only put the tie round his neck. It didn't *do* anything. Gus could have much more fun with it!

"*Gus!*"

At the sound of Mrs Carter's stern voice behind him, Gus suddenly decided that he'd had enough fun with Mr Carter's tie after all. He let go, and Holly fell backwards, landing on her bottom.

"Oh no! It *would* be his favourite tie!" Mrs Carter stared sternly at the puppy. "You're a very naughty boy, Gus!"

Gus decided it was time for his best "I'm sorry" look. He slumped down and put his head on his paws. His big brown eyes looked sadly up at Mrs Carter and Holly.

"Oh, isn't he sweet?" Holly knelt down and cuddled him. Gus wagged his tail joyfully and rolled over to let her tickle his fat little tummy.

"He's a monster," Mrs Carter said, but she was trying not to smile. "Here, Holly, you'd better go and put this in the bin. And let's hope your dad doesn't notice it's gone. He still hasn't realised his leather gloves have disappeared too."

Gus wondered if they'd found Mr Carter's slippers – the ones he'd hidden behind the sofa to have a quiet chew on when he was bored. He hoped not. He'd hardly started on the left one yet.

Holly went downstairs with the remains of the tie, and Gus raced after her. He was hungry, and he was sure it was time for his next meal. He bounced into the kitchen and sat down hopefully by his empty bowl.

"Oh, Gus!" sighed Mrs Carter as she followed them in. "You can't be hungry again." She looked at the clock. "You only had your lunch half an hour ago!"

Gus couldn't understand what the round thing on the wall had to do with whether he was fed or not. He glared up at it, wishing he could reach it – he'd chew it to bits!

"Here, Gus," Holly whispered, slipping him a dog biscuit while her mother was busy at the sink. Gus wolfed it down gratefully and gave her a big lick on the nose. Holly giggled and hugged him.

"That dog could win a gold medal for eating!" Mrs Carter shook her head as she turned on the taps. "And what he doesn't eat, he chews!"

But I'm hungry! Gus thought grumpily. He barked a few times, but Mrs Carter shook her head.

"No, Gus. You've had quite enough."

"No, I haven't," Gus woofed to himself. He waited until Mrs Carter and Holly were busy doing the washing-up, then he trotted out of the kitchen door into the back garden.

It was a warm sunny day, but Gus didn't even stop to chase the butterflies. He hurried over to the fence and wriggled through a small gap he'd found into Mr Smith's garden.

Mr Smith was sitting in a deckchair with a plate of cheese sandwiches on his knee. Gus was delighted. He loved cheese sandwiches. He bounded over to Mr Smith, barking a greeting.

"Hello, Gus." The old man put down his newspaper and patted the puppy on the head. "How did you know I was having my lunch? You always arrive at just the right moment!"

Gus shared Mr Smith's plate of cheese sandwiches, then he said goodbye and went next door to the Burtons' house.

Emma, who was in Holly's class at school, was playing in the garden with her little brother Paul. Jock, their

Westie, was there too. Emma and Paul were eating salt and vinegar crisps. Gus's favourite flavour was cheese and onion, but he liked salt and vinegar too, so he hurried over to them.

"Oh no, not you again!" Jock barked, as Emma and Paul made a big fuss of Gus. "Doesn't Holly feed you?"

"Of course she does!" Gus growled as he crunched up all the crisps the children were giving him. "But I'm still hungry!"

Gus stayed until all the crisps were finished, then moved on. Mr Graham, who lived at Number 7, wasn't at home, but Gus got some chicken from

Mrs Patel at Number 9 and a rusk from the baby at Number 11.

By now, Gus was beginning to feel quite full. He decided it was time to go home. There was only one house left in the row anyway, and it wasn't on Gus's usual round. Mrs Wilson, who lived at Number 13, didn't like dogs. Instead she had a snooty white Persian cat called Lulu, who walked up and down the street with her nose in the air.

Gus was about to head for home when he smelt something. He stopped in his tracks and sniffed. He sniffed again. It was a delicious smell, warm and fruity and spicy. And it was coming from Mrs Wilson's house.

Gus had to find out what it was. He hurried back across the lawn of Number 11 to look for a gap in the fence he'd noticed, leading into Mrs Wilson's garden.

It was rather a squeeze, but Gus managed to push his way through. The kitchen door stood open, and the smell was getting stronger and more delicious by the minute.

Gus crept up to the doorway and peeped inside. He didn't want to meet Mrs Wilson or Lulu. But the kitchen was empty.

Something was bubbling away in a

big pan on top of the cooker and, on the big wooden table, Gus could see a big cake and lots of little pies and tarts, cooling on a wire rack.

Licking his lips, Gus padded softly into the kitchen. He jumped up onto one of the kitchen chairs and put his paws on the table. He didn't know where to start! As well as the cake, there were custard tarts – another of Gus's favourites. And next to a big bowl of pastry mix with a wooden spoon stuck in it, Gus spotted chocolate chip cookies!

But the big sponge cake with jam in the middle was nearest. Just as Gus opened his mouth to take a big bite out of it, Mrs Wilson walked into the kitchen with Lulu in her arms.

"*Eeek!*" Mrs Wilson screamed when she saw Gus. "Get away from my cake, you horrid little dog!"

"How dare you come into my house!" Lulu hissed at him, showing her sharp teeth.

Frightened, Gus jumped down and ran for the door. He rushed back through the gap in the fence into Number 11's garden, and through all the other gardens, not stopping until he was safely back home.

"Gus, I've been looking for you!" Holly said as Gus trotted into the

kitchen. "Where've you been?"

"I can guess," said Mrs Carter. "On his usual round of visits to the neighbours!"

"Gus, have you been begging for food again?" Holly asked sternly.

Gus opened his eyes wide and tried to look as if he'd never dream of doing such a thing.

Holly couldn't help laughing. "You're a bad boy!" she said, stroking his soft coat.

"It's lucky our neighbours like him," Mrs Carter remarked, "or they'd be complaining all the time!"

Right at that moment Mrs Wilson

burst in through the kitchen door, making everyone, including Gus, jump. She was red in the face and looked very upset indeed.

"Is something wrong, Mrs Wilson?" Holly asked.

"Yes, something's very wrong!" Mrs Wilson said angrily. "I want to complain about your dog. He's eaten my diamond ring!"

Chapter Two

"*What?*" gasped Holly and Mrs Carter together.

Gus looked puzzled. He didn't even know what a diamond ring was. But whatever it was, he was sure he hadn't eaten it. He hadn't eaten anything in Mrs Wilson's kitchen.

"He's eaten my diamond ring!"

Mrs Wilson said again.

"Gus wouldn't eat a *ring*," Holly said.

"Why not?" Mrs Wilson snapped. "That dog eats anything! He ate all the heads off my daffodils once!"

"And they tasted *horrible*!" Gus barked indignantly.

"Gus, be quiet!" said Mrs Carter. Then she turned to Mrs Wilson. "Why do you think Gus is to blame, Mrs Wilson?" she asked.

"Because I found him climbing onto my kitchen table about five minutes ago!" Mrs Wilson said crossly. "I'd taken my ring off and left it on the table while I was baking. When I

came back, it was gone!"

Mrs Wilson suddenly looked very sad. "The ring was a present from my husband," she said quietly. "It's very precious to me. I simply *must* get it back."

"I'm sorry, Mrs Wilson," Holly said.

"But I'm sure Gus didn't eat your ring."

Gus licked Holly's hand gratefully.

Mrs Wilson shook her head. "He *must* have done!" she declared.

"It *wasn't* me!" Gus howled. "Your stuck-up cat could have eaten the ring!"

"Be *quiet*, Gus!" Mrs Carter said sharply.

Gus shut up. He hadn't seen Holly's mum get quite so angry before, and it scared him.

"I suppose Gus *might* have eaten the ring," Mrs Carter said slowly. "He does like to eat very odd things sometimes."

"Oh, *Mum!*" Holly said. "Gus wouldn't eat a diamond ring. Not if there were cakes and biscuits lying about."

"He would have hoovered up everything on the table if I hadn't walked in just then!" Mrs Wilson said furiously. "That dog's a menace!"

Gus couldn't be quiet any longer, and he barked loudly. It wasn't fair! He hadn't eaten Mrs Wilson's nasty old ring, and he didn't see why he should get the blame.

"Gus, be *quiet!*" shouted Mrs Carter. "Holly, go and shut him in the living room while I talk to Mrs Wilson."

"That dog needs to be taught some manners!" Mrs Wilson sniffed.

"Sit down, Mrs Wilson, and I'll make

you a nice cup of tea," Holly's mum said. "Then we can talk about how we can find your ring."

Holly took Gus's collar and pulled him out of the kitchen. Gus dug his claws in because he didn't want to leave. He wanted to stay there and tell Mrs Wilson exactly what he thought of her. But in the end he gave in, and let Holly take him into the living room.

"Oh, Gus," Holly sighed, kneeling down to put her arms around him. "I wish you hadn't gone into Mrs Wilson's kitchen."

"So do I," Gus woofed miserably as he snuggled into her arms. "Then I wouldn't be in this mess!"

"If only you could talk!" Holly went on, looking just as miserable. "Then you could tell us what really happened."

Gus whined, and put his paw on Holly's arm. He hated to see her so sad. And it was all his fault. That made him feel even worse.

"I'll go and see what Mum and Mrs Wilson are saying," Holly told him. "Be a good boy, Gus, and don't make a noise."

She went out, closing the door behind her. Gus slumped down on the carpet and put his nose between his paws. He felt very sad indeed. If only he hadn't been so greedy, none of this would have happened. Now he had made Holly unhappy – and he'd made Mrs Carter very angry.

Suddenly Gus sat up, feeling frightened. What if Mrs Carter was *so* angry with him that he was sent back to the Dogs' Home? Gus had been born at the home and had lived there until, one day, the Carters had come looking for a puppy and had chosen him. That had been the happiest day of Gus's life.

The Dogs' Home was big and noisy and crowded. The people there were very busy. They didn't have time to play with him like Holly did. Gus didn't want to go back there. Besides, he loved Holly more than anyone else in the whole world, and he didn't want to leave her. So there was only one thing to do . . .

Gus jumped up. He must find Mrs Wilson's diamond ring himself, and show everyone that he hadn't eaten it!

Chapter Three

Gus looked round the living room, wondering how he could get out. The door was closed, but one of the windows was open just a little. Gus knew he wasn't allowed on the furniture, but this was an emergency. He leapt onto the big armchair near the window and scrambled up its back and onto the windowsill.

Gus nudged the window open a little wider with his nose and looked out. It seemed an awfully long way down and he felt rather nervous about jumping. But then Gus remembered Holly's sad face. He took a deep breath, jumped . . .

. . . and landed safely in the soft earth of the flowerbed beneath the window.

"Yes!" he barked proudly. "I did it!"

Gus picked himself up and trotted down the garden path. There was no time to waste. He had to get to Mrs Wilson's house and find the ring before something awful happened to him.

"Hey, Gus!" Jock was in the Burtons' back garden, chewing on a large juicy bone. He looked up as Gus raced past. "Do you want a lick? There's plenty here for two!"

Gus shook his head. "I'm not hungry!" he called, and didn't stop. He didn't care if he never saw a bone again, as long as he didn't have to leave Holly and go back to the Dogs' Home.

Jock was so surprised he dropped the bone. It rolled into the Burtons' fish pond, and Jock didn't even notice. "Gus isn't hungry?" he barked. "I don't believe it!"

When Gus reached the gap in the fence leading to Mrs Wilson's garden he skidded to a halt, panting hard. Then he squeezed through the gap and trotted up the path to the kitchen door, looking carefully around him in case Mrs Wilson was already on her way back home.

But this time the kitchen door was closed. Gus's heart sank. He should have guessed that Mrs Wilson would lock up her house before she left. But he had to find a way in. He had to.

Keeping a nervous lookout for Lulu, Gus went to investigate the back of the house. Gus wasn't the only dog in the street who was scared of Lulu. He'd seen the hefty white cat take on dogs before. She sent them running home with their tails between their legs as soon as she lashed out with her razor-sharp claws. But luckily Lulu was nowhere to be seen.

All the windows at the back of the house were closed. Gus ran up and down trying to find a way in, but there was not even a tiny gap he could squeeze through.

Gloomily Gus went back to the kitchen door again. What was he going to do? Somehow he had to get into that house, or he might be back in the Dogs' Home before he could say "Woof". And then he'd never see Holly again . . .

Gus whined and stood up on his back legs, putting his front paws on the kitchen door. He pushed at it as hard as he could, but it didn't move. It was then that Gus noticed something at the bottom of the door. Lulu's cat flap!

Gus was so excited that he had to stop himself from barking out loud. Eagerly he pushed his nose against the flap. It moved, and Gus stuck his head through into Mrs Wilson's kitchen. Now for the rest of him . . .

Carefully Gus began to make his way through the hole in the door. He wriggled and he pushed and he just about got his front paws and shoulders inside. It was a very tight fit.

Gus tried to get his other half through the cat flap. He wriggled and he pulled, but he couldn't move. He tried again and again, but his tummy was too big to get through the hole. He was stuck!

Gus began to feel very frightened. He didn't know what to do. He couldn't get in and he couldn't get out.

Then behind him he heard a silky voice say, "And what do you think you're doing in *my* cat flap?"

Chapter Four

It was Lulu! Gus began to tremble with fear.

"You look very silly indeed," Lulu said. Gus could almost hear her sharpening her claws gleefully. "I think you'd better come out, right now."

"I can't!" Gus whined miserably. "I'm stuck!"

"Serves you right for eating the diamond ring!" Lulu sniffed.

"I *didn't* eat it!" Gus said indignantly. "I've come to look for it. And – and I've got to find it because if I don't, I might get sent back to the Dogs' Home and then I'll never see Holly again . . ."

Lulu didn't say anything, and Gus began to feel even more nervous. He couldn't see what the cat was doing behind him, but he didn't want to stay and find out. He began to wriggle about again, trying to get through the cat flap into Mrs Wilson's kitchen.

"Keep still!" Lulu hissed at him. "You'll never get in that way – you're too fat! You'd better try and come out again."

Gus knew that Lulu was right. He was just too big to get through the cat flap. "But I can't get out again either!" he wailed.

"Yes, you can!" Lulu said crossly. "You got in, didn't you? Just take it slowly."

Gus began trying to ease himself gently backwards. At first he didn't move at all. He pulled harder . . . and harder . . . Then, all of a sudden, he shot backwards out of the cat flap like a cork out of a bottle, and tumbled head over heels onto the path.

"Thank you!" he woofed.

Lulu, who was having a wash, gave him a bored look. "Dogs!" she yawned. "They're so stupid! I can show you a much better way to get into the house."

Gus stared at the cat in amazement.

"You want to get into the house, don't you?" Lulu jumped onto a dustbin which stood underneath the kitchen windows. She began pulling at the smallest window with her claws and, after a minute or two, it swung open.

"The catch is broken," explained Lulu as she leapt down onto the path again. "If you can get up there, you can climb into the kitchen quite easily."

Gus could hardly believe his ears. Lulu, the cat who hated dogs, was helping him?

"Thank you!" he said. "But – but why are you helping me like this?"

"I came from the Cats' Home," Lulu said quietly. "I wouldn't want to go back there either!"

The dustbin was quite tall, but there was a big black bag of rubbish lying next to it. Gus climbed onto the bag first and then managed to get onto the dustbin. From there, it was easy for him to jump up onto the windowsill.

He peered through the window into Mrs Wilson's kitchen. Just below him was the sink and draining board, which was piled with clean plates and cups.

Gus hopped down carefully onto the edge of the sink, but felt his front paw skidding on the slippery surface. *CRASH!*

As Gus knocked against the pile of crockery, plates and cups flew everywhere and smashed to bits as they hit the floor.

"I think that's called a crash landing," Lulu remarked as she came in through the cat flap.

"Oh, no!" Gus muttered. "How did *that* happen?" He inspected his paw. He'd trodden on a drop of spilt washing-up liquid. No wonder he'd slipped!

He jumped down off the draining board. It wasn't a very good start. Still, he was sure Mrs Wilson would forgive him if he found her diamond ring.

"Where are you going to start

looking?" Lulu asked.

"I . . . er . . . don't quite know." Gus suddenly realised that he didn't even know what a diamond ring was.

Lulu sighed. "You do *know* what a diamond ring is, don't you?"

"No," said Gus sadly.

Lulu told him. Gus couldn't help feeling alarmed when he found out how small it was. He looked around the enormous kitchen. How would he find a tiny little thing like a diamond ring in here? But he had to try, for Holly's sake.

First Gus went over to the kitchen table. He remembered that Mrs Wilson said she'd left her ring there when she'd started cooking. All the cakes and biscuits and the big bowl of pastry mix were still there, but Gus wasn't interested in food. He jumped up onto a chair and nosed around, looking for the ring.

CRASH! Lulu jumped as Gus accidentally knocked the plate of chocolate chip cookies onto the floor.

"Be careful!" she hissed.

Gus didn't care. He had to find that ring. But there was no sign of it on the kitchen table.

Next Gus sniffed his way all round the kitchen floor, in case the ring had fallen off the table. It hadn't.

Then he looked in all the cupboards

he could reach. It wasn't easy, because it took him a long time to get each one open. The cupboards were so full of tins, bottles and packets of food that things kept falling out onto the floor.

Meanwhile, Lulu looked in all the places Gus couldn't reach, like the top of the fridge and the high shelves on the wall. But they didn't find the ring.

"It's not here!" Gus slumped down miserably on the kitchen floor. "What am I going to do?"

"We'd better get out of here," Lulu said, looking around the kitchen, "or we're going to be in big trouble."

Gus looked around the kitchen too,

and his heart sank. It was a mess. The floor was covered with bits of broken crockery and cookies, along with tins and packets of food. What on earth would Mrs Wilson say when she saw it?

Lulu was right. They had to get out of there, and fast – before Mrs Wilson came back.

Then, suddenly, Gus's ears pricked up. He could hear Holly's voice! He

listened harder. Now he could hear Mrs Carter and Mrs Wilson talking as well. The voices were coming closer and closer. Gus could hear footsteps too.

Mrs Wilson and Holly and her mum were walking up the path to Mrs Wilson's kitchen door!

Gus panicked. He ran over to the sink, but the draining board was too high for him to jump onto.

"Hide!" Lulu hissed, her tail swinging wildly from side to side.

Gus looked frantically around for somewhere to hide, but it was too late. The voices were already outside the back door!

Chapter Five

"But I've looked *everywhere*," Mrs Wilson was saying, as she put her key into the lock. "I tell you, that puppy of yours *must* have eaten it!"

"Gus can be a bit naughty at times, Mrs Wilson," Holly admitted, "but I'm *sure* he wouldn't have eaten your ring."

"Let's have another look for it," Mrs

Carter added. "Holly and I will help you."

"It won't do any good," Mrs Wilson sniffed, sounding rather tearful as she pushed open the kitchen door. "I know exactly where my ring is – inside your dog's tummy! I'm never going to get it back . . ." The door swung open.

"Oh, no!" Mrs Wilson stopped dead in the doorway. "Look at my kitchen!" she wailed.

"Well, everyone makes a bit of a mess when they're baking," said Mrs Carter, trying not to look shocked.

"I didn't do this!" Mrs Wilson cried. "Ooh! And look at all my crockery!"

she shouted, as she noticed the mess by the sink.

Then suddenly she spotted Gus, who was trying to hide under the kitchen table. "Aha! I might have known!" Her face red with fury, Mrs Wilson bent down under the table, grabbed Gus's collar and pulled him out.

"Gus!" Holly gasped. "How on earth did you get in here?"

Gus whined. He was in real trouble now.

"Never mind how he got in here!" Mrs Wilson retorted, still keeping a tight hold of Gus's collar. "Somehow he did, and just *look* at the mess he's made. *And* he's scared my cat!"

Lulu, who was sitting on top of the fridge watching what was going on, miaowed loudly. "He didn't scare *me!*" she said, offended that anyone could think she found a mere puppy scary.

"I'm so sorry, Mrs Wilson," said Holly's mum quickly. "I just don't understand how Gus got in. We'll pay for the damage, of course."

"Maybe he came to look for the ring," Holly said.

"Oh, very funny!" snorted Mrs Wilson rudely.

"Don't be silly, Holly," said her mum.

"I'm not!" Holly insisted. "Maybe Gus was just trying to help."

Gus gave a yelp. At least Holly believed in him. He tried to pull away from Mrs Wilson, so that he could rush over to Holly and give her another grateful lick, but Mrs Wilson was holding his collar too tightly. In fact, she was holding it so tightly, it was beginning to hurt. Gus pulled harder, trying to get away.

"Now I want to know what you're going to do about this . . . this animal!" Mrs Wilson demanded. "He's eaten my precious ring and messed up my kitchen, and I've just about had enough!"

Gus made one last effort to get away from Mrs Wilson. Dragging her with him, Gus lunged forward towards Holly.

"Aah!" Mrs Wilson screamed again as she fell against the table. The bowl of pastry mix toppled off and hit the floor with a great clatter. Big splodges of sticky yellow pastry mix flew everywhere, especially over Gus and Mrs Wilson.

"Look what he's done!" Mrs Wilson spluttered furiously as she tried to wipe the pastry crumbs off her face. "That dog should be locked up – he's dangerous!"

"Oh, Gus!" Holly sighed. "What have you done *now*?"

But Gus wasn't listening. He could see something glittering in the pastry mix on the floor.

Chapter Six

"I want that dog out of my kitchen *now*!" Mrs Wilson shouted angrily.

"Come on, Gus." Holly hurried across the kitchen towards him. "I think we'd better go."

Gus took no notice. He pushed his nose into the heap of pastry mix and barked loudly.

Holly knelt down beside him. "What are you doing, Gus?" she asked.

Gus barked again and scrabbled in the pastry mix with his paws.

Then Holly suddenly saw what he was trying to show her. "It's the ring!" she shouted, picking it up. "Gus has found the ring!"

"*What*?" Mrs Wilson's eyes almost popped out of her head. "Let me see that!"

She grabbed the sticky, pastry-covered ring, rushed over to the tap and rinsed it clean. "It *is* my ring! Oh, thank goodness," she said in a shaky voice. "I thought it had gone for ever!"

"It must have fallen into the bowl of pastry mix!" said Mrs Carter.

"It's a good job you didn't make that pastry into pies, Mrs Wilson," said Holly. "The ring would have been inside, and someone might have *really* eaten it!"

Mrs Wilson turned pale at the very thought and had to sit down on one of the kitchen chairs.

"Well done, Gus!" Holly said proudly, giving her puppy a big hug. "We'd never have found the ring if it wasn't for you!"

Gus began to bark joyfully. Thank goodness he'd managed to get himself out of trouble. But it had been a close thing!

Mrs Wilson looked round at the mess in her kitchen and frowned. "It was really very naughty of you to come into my kitchen, Gus," she said.

Gus hung his head. If he hadn't been so greedy in the first place, none of this would have happened.

Then Mrs Wilson smiled. "But it was very clever of you to find my ring!" She slipped the ring onto her finger, then bent down and patted Gus on the head.

Gus licked her hand. Maybe now he and Mrs Wilson could be friends.

"We'll help you clean up the kitchen,

Mrs Wilson," said Holly.

Mrs Wilson looked pleased. "Thank you, Holly," she said.

Holly and her mum helped to tidy up. Then, carrying the big wedges of jam sponge Mrs Wilson had cut and wrapped for them, along with a pile of chocolate chip cookies, they said goodbye.

"From now on, there will always be a little something for you here, when you're feeling peckish, Gus," Mrs

Wilson said. "It's the least I can do!"

"Yippee!" Gus barked happily.

"Just don't get any ideas about scoffing my cat food," Lulu purred quietly from the top of the fridge.

When they got back home, Mrs Carter went straight over to the fridge and took out a big, juicy bone. "I think Gus deserves a reward for finding Mrs Wilson's ring!" she said with a smile.

"So do I!" said Holly. She took the bone and held it out to Gus. "Here you are, Gus! Good boy!"

Holly and her mum couldn't believe their eyes when Gus ignored the bone.

Instead he flung himself at Holly, licking her hand and wagging his tail.

"Oh, Gus!" Holly laughed, dropping the bone and scooping her puppy into her arms. "Aren't you hungry?"

"Of course he's hungry!" Mrs Carter laughed. "Gus is always hungry!"

But for once, Gus didn't care about the big, juicy bone. He was just glad to be back home safely, with Holly.

If he hadn't found Mrs Wilson's ring, he might have been on his way back to the Dogs' Home right now . . .

. . . *And if I hadn't been so greedy in the first place, I wouldn't have got into so much trouble*, Gus thought. *I'm not going*

to be so greedy ANY MORE!

"I really don't think Gus wants this bone, Mum," said Holly.

Mrs Carter looked surprised. "Oh well, put it back in the fridge, and he can have it later," she said. "Maybe Gus has decided to change his ways!"

"I have!" Gus yapped happily as Holly gave him a cuddle. "I still love food, but not as much as I love you, Holly!"

He gave her a lick, then looked at her hopefully. "But when my appetite comes back," he woofed, "I'd be more than happy to help out with that jam sponge!"

Spot
the Sporty Puppy

Special thanks to Narinder Dhami

To Reba – another sporty puppy!

Chapter One

"Fetch the ball, Spot!"

Spot went chasing across the field. He grabbed the squeaky ball in his teeth and raced back to Matt. The ball made a dreadful noise as he ran.

"Good boy, Spot!" Matt, Spot's owner, knelt down and stroked his Dalmatian puppy's silky black-and-white ears. "You're a really fast runner!"

Spot wagged his tail proudly and licked Matt's hand. Spot loved running nearly as much as he loved Matt. He would put his ears back and race from one end of the field to the other, feeling the wind rushing past him and ruffling his fur. It was better than a big, juicy bone, or even a roll in a dirty puddle.

Matt looked at his watch. "Time to go home, Spot, or I'm going to be late for school."

Spot whined grumpily. He didn't want to go home yet. Every morning Matt took him for a long walk in the playing field behind their house, where

Spot met up with some of the other dogs that lived in their street. They usually had races and Spot, of course, always won. But this morning Matt seemed in a hurry.

"Sorry, Spot," Matt said, as he clipped the lead to his puppy's collar. "I promise I'll take you out for a longer walk tonight."

Spot woofed. He didn't really mind going home because he had a special secret. A *very* special secret. When Matt was at school and Mrs Robinson, Matt's mum, was at work, Spot could run around the field as much as he liked!

Matt and Spot went across the field

to the Robinsons' back gate.

Matt opened it and then closed it carefully behind them. "Come on, Spot! Race you to the kitchen!"

Spot dashed up the garden path, his white tail wagging furiously from side to side, and got to the open kitchen door just before Matt did. He dived into the kitchen and skidded across the floor, stopping with expert timing in front of his empty bowl.

"You're just in time for breakfast, Spot!" laughed Mrs Robinson, who was spreading butter on toast. She shook some dog biscuits into the bowl and Spot began to crunch them noisily.

"You won, Spot!" Matt said with a grin. "Mum, did you wash my kit ready for Sports Day this afternoon?"

Spot stopped eating and pricked up his ears. Did Matt say *Spot's* Day?

Matt saw Spot looking eagerly up at him and smiled. "No, not *Spot's* Day – *Sports* Day!"

Spot didn't know what Sports Day was, so he wasn't very interested. He went back to eating his biscuits.

"You *are* coming to watch, aren't you, Mum?" Matt asked.

Mrs Robinson nodded. "I'll be home from work at lunchtime, so I'll be there to cheer you on."

"Great!" said Matt. "I'm going to try really hard to win one of the races this year!"

Spot's ears pricked up again when he heard the word *race*. He still didn't know what Sports Day was, but he was beginning to like the sound of it! He hoped that he would be allowed to go this afternoon too.

"Time to go, Matt," said Mrs Robinson.

Spot dashed over to the kitchen door, and barked.

"Do you want to stay in the garden this morning, Spot?" asked Mrs Robinson with a smile.

Spot barked again, so she carried the puppy's bowls outside and gave him some more biscuits and some fresh water. "Matt, you did shut the back gate properly, didn't you?" she asked. "We don't want Spot getting out."

Matt nodded. "Bye, Spot. See you later."

Spot waited until he heard the car start up and drive away, taking Mrs Robinson to work and Matt to school.

Then he scampered eagerly to the other end of the garden. He scrabbled about at the bottom of the hedge and uncovered his secret – a small hole. He squeezed his way through, and then he was out in the playing field again.

Spot ran joyfully across the grass, sniffing the air as he went. He knew he wasn't really allowed out on his own, but he got so bored at home when Matt was at school. This way he could meet up with all his other friends!

He ran about on his own for a while, scrabbling in the hedgerows and finding lots of interesting smells. Then he saw Jasper the black Labrador, who lived a few doors away from the Robinsons. Jasper was out with his owner, Mr Smith.

Spot bounded up to him and gave him a friendly nudge with his nose. "Come on, I'll race you to the other end of the field!" he barked.

"Oh no, not again!" Jasper groaned. "You always beat me!"

"Hello, Spot." Mr Smith bent down and patted the Dalmatian. "You're out on your own again, I see!"

Spot woofed and wagged his tail. He hoped Mr Smith wouldn't say anything to the Robinsons, or his special secret would be discovered!

Spot and Jasper set off across the field. Spot was soon in front and he won the race easily, before Jasper had even run halfway. The Labrador gave up, panting.

"You shouldn't eat so many biscuits!" Spot yapped at him. "Then you'd be able to run as fast as me!"

Jasper lay down and put his nose between his paws. "I need a rest!" he whined.

Spot suddenly thought of something. "Jasper, do you know what *Sports Day* is?"

"It's a special day for children at school," Jasper woofed back. "They have lots of races, and all the mums and dads go to watch."

Spot's eyes lit up. A moment later he was running away across the field again.

"Where are you going?" Jasper barked after him.

"Home!" Spot barked back. "I don't want to miss Sports Day!"

It seemed a very long time to Spot before Mrs Robinson arrived home at lunchtime. He jumped around, whining impatiently, as she opened the back door.

"Hello, Spot!" She patted him, then checked that he still had water in his bowl. "I've got to rush – I'm late for Sports Day!"

Spot began to bark at the top of his voice, feeling very excited. He could hardly wait to go and join in all the races!

"No, you can't come, I'm afraid, Spot," said Matt's mum, and she quickly locked the back door again.

Spot slumped miserably on the grass. *Why* couldn't he go to Sports Day? After all, he was the fastest dog in the street! If there were races going on, he ought to be allowed to take part in them . . .

Spot's ears pricked up. He could hear voices. Lots of them. It sounded as if there were suddenly lots of people in the playing field.

He hurried down to the end of the garden and looked through his secret hole in the hedge.

There *were* lots of people in the field.

And there were some strange, exciting things happening too. Balloons and streamers had been tied up in the trees. There were lots of chairs laid out in rows, as well as a small platform with people standing on it.

Spot was puzzled. Who were all these

people, and what was going on?

Then, to his delight, Spot saw Matt! The puppy could hardly believe his eyes. So *this* must be Sports Day! And it was happening right there, in his own playing field! Spot only had to squeeze through the secret hole to go and join in the fun. And that was just what he was going to do!

Chapter Two

Spot was so excited it took him a moment or two to wriggle his way through the hole in the hedge. But at last, he did it. He raced happily across the field towards the crowd of people, hoping he hadn't missed any of the races. But nothing much seemed to be happening, except that a man was standing on the little platform, talking to the parents and children who sat in rows on either side of him.

". . . And as headmaster of Redhill Primary School, it gives me great pleasure to welcome all of you here to Sports Day," the man was saying. "We'll start with the special teachers' race. All the teachers will be taking part, including myself!"

Spot had heard Matt talking about the headmaster. His name was Mr Brown and Matt was a bit scared of him because he was very strict. As people clapped the headmaster's speech, Spot bared his teeth and growled a little. He hoped Mr Brown didn't win!

Nobody noticed the puppy as he looked around for Matt. The teachers were lining up at the top of the track for the start of the race. There were two children standing at the bottom end, holding a tape stretched out between them. That was the finishing-line.

Spot felt very excited. How wonderful it would feel to be the first to cross the line and win! All these people would jump up and cheer, and Matt would be very proud of him . . .

"Spot! What on earth are *you* doing here?"

Spot's heart sank. Mrs Robinson had

seen him! She had jumped up from her seat and was hurrying across the grass towards him. She didn't look very pleased, either.

Spot knew very well that if he was caught he'd be taken home again, so he scurried off as fast as his legs could carry him.

"Spot, you naughty boy!" Mrs Robinson called. "Come back!"

Spot pretended he hadn't heard. He decided to find a place to hide and wriggled under a row of chairs, squeezing his way around people's legs.

Some of the people leant down and tried to grab him as he rushed by. But

Spot managed to wriggle away from them.

Just then, Mrs Williams, the school secretary, shouted, "On your marks! Get set! *Go!*"

The teachers' race had started! Spot crawled forward to sit under a chair in the front row, right next to the track. He poked his head out to see what was going on.

The teachers were all charging across the grass towards the finishing-line. Mr Brown was in the lead and he looked determined to win.

Spot wondered if the other teachers were letting Mr Brown win because he was the headmaster. He wished *he* had a chance to race against Mr Brown – he was sure he could beat him.

"Spot!"

That was Matt's voice. Spot sat up eagerly and looked around.

"Spot!"

Then Spot saw his owner. Matt was dressed in his sports kit and was standing on the opposite side of the track with his best friend, Daniel Parsons.

Spot was so excited he dashed out from under the chair where he was hiding and across the track. At exactly the same moment the teachers came running at full speed towards him, Mr Brown still in the lead.

Spot had no time to get out of the way. Neither did the headmaster. They crashed into each other with a yelp and a shout. Mr Brown tripped over Spot and went flying head over heels, landing in a heap on the grass!

Chapter Three

"What . . . who . . . ?" spluttered Mr Brown in a dazed voice, as he pulled himself to his feet. "What is this . . . this *animal* doing here?"

Spot cowered in the grass, feeling very frightened. He hadn't meant to trip up Mr Brown. The headmaster looked very big and menacing as he towered over

Spot. The puppy was glad when Matt rushed over and picked him up.

"Sorry, sir," Matt said breathlessly. "He's mine."

"And what's he doing at Sports Day?" Mr Brown glared down at Spot, who huddled even closer to Matt. "No dogs are allowed!"

"He must have got out of our back garden somehow," Matt explained quickly. "We live just there." He pointed to his house.

Mr Brown opened his mouth to say something else, then changed his mind. He'd noticed that some of the children and their parents were laughing, and even the teachers who'd now finished the race were trying not to smile.

"Well, get rid of him then," he snapped. "And quickly!"

Spot whimpered as Matt hurried across the track towards his mum. The parents and children who were watching were still laughing and pointing at them. Spot felt very ashamed of himself.

"It's OK, Spot," Matt whispered quietly into his puppy's ear. "Thanks to you, my teacher Miss Marshall won the race!"

Spot looked up at Matt and gave him a grateful lick on the chin. He felt a bit better now. Then Spot saw the look on Mrs Robinson's face . . .

"You're a very bad boy, Spot!" she scolded as Matt handed the puppy to her. "You could have caused a serious accident!"

Spot whimpered anxiously and tried to lick her hand.

"This is your fault as well, Matt," Mrs Robinson went on. "You can't have closed the back gate properly this morning, and Spot must have got out."

Spot felt terrible when he heard that. He didn't want Matt to be blamed when it wasn't his fault. He began to whine loudly, but stopped as he saw Mr Brown glaring at him again.

"I'd better take Spot home right away," Mrs Robinson sighed, "before he can do any more damage!"

Matt's face fell. "But if you go now, you'll miss my first race!" he said. "It's the egg and spoon."

Mrs Robinson hesitated. "Well, all

right. I'll stay and watch that first."

Spot's tail began to wag a little. At least he was going to see Matt take part in *one* race!

"You'd better behave yourself now, Spot," Mrs Robinson said firmly, as she sat down with the puppy on her lap. "I think Mr Brown's had enough of you for one day!"

"Hello, Spot!" said the woman who was sitting next to Mrs Robinson.

Spot knew who she was and wagged his tail. It was Mrs Parsons, Daniel's mum, and she had Daniel's little sister Emma in her arms.

"Dog!" said Emma, trying to grab

Spot's ear. "Dog! Woof, woof!"

Spot licked her hand, and Emma squealed with delight.

"Look, Emma," said Mrs Parsons, lifting the little girl up. "There's Daniel and Matt!"

Spot looked up the track too, and saw Matt and his friend lining up for the egg and spoon race. Spot wasn't sure what an egg and spoon race was. Did the children have to eat the egg with the spoon?

"On your marks!" shouted Mr Brown, who was starting off the race.

Spot was amazed to see that all the children, including Matt, were holding a spoon with an egg balanced on it.

"Get set!" shouted Mr Brown. "*Go!*"

The race began. The children set off, half-running and half-walking, carefully holding their eggs and spoons in front of them.

Spot watched, puzzled. What a strange race! But he began to get excited when he saw that Matt was in the lead!

"Come on, Matt!" shouted Mrs Robinson, bouncing Spot up and down on her knee.

Spot barked loudly, straining forward to get a better view. Matt was still in the lead, running along very carefully, his eyes fixed on the egg in front of him.

But then, just as Matt drew level with Mrs Robinson and Spot, he stumbled. The egg fell off his spoon into the grass.

Matt's mum had got so excited watching the race that she'd loosened her grip on Spot. Spot didn't hesitate. He leapt off her lap and dashed across the grass to pick up the egg. If he took it to the finishing-line, Matt might still win!

The other children taking part in the race were so surprised to see Spot darting in front of them that they all dropped their eggs too. Spot ignored them and grabbed Matt's egg in his teeth.

The egg was surprisingly hard and

168

shiny. It felt more like a stone or a pebble. Spot decided it couldn't be a real egg, after all.

"Spot!" Matt was running towards him. "Come here!"

Spot galloped off towards the finishing-line, making sure that Matt was following him. He dashed under the tape and was thrilled to hear cheers from the crowd.

Matt followed him a few seconds later. They'd won! Spot danced around Matt's ankles, barking loudly with delight.

"This dog is ruining our Sports Day!" boomed an angry voice.

Everyone fell silent as Mr Brown, panting and red in the face, hurried down the track towards Matt and Spot.

Alarmed, Spot hid behind Matt's legs, trying to make himself as small as possible. He'd done the wrong thing *again.* But he'd only wanted to help Matt win a race!

"I'm terribly sorry, Mr Brown," said Mrs Robinson, as she rushed over and picked Spot up. "I'll take him home right away."

"Thank you," snapped the headmaster. "I think we'd better run the race again – and this time we'll do it properly!"

Spot looked miserably over Mrs Robinson's shoulder as she carried him away from all the fun. He'd got Matt into trouble again, and they hadn't even won the race in the end. It looked as if Sports Day was over for Spot.

Chapter Four

"In you go, Spot." Mrs Robinson swung open the back gate and took the puppy inside the garden. She frowned. "Why isn't the gate still open? Oh, well, the wind must have blown it shut after you'd got out."

She wagged her finger sternly at Spot. "Now you behave yourself until we get back!"

Spot sat on the grass and looked up at Mrs Robinson, his brown eyes miserable.

Mrs Robinson couldn't help smiling. "It's all right, Spot," she said, giving him a pat. "I know you didn't mean any harm. Be a good boy, now. We'll be home soon."

She went out again, checking the gate to make sure it was properly shut.

Gloomily, Spot lay down and put his nose between his paws. He'd really made a mess of things this time. He'd got Matt into trouble with his mum *and* with his headmaster.

Suddenly the people in the field started cheering loudly. Spot couldn't help himself. He dashed straight over to his secret hole to see what was going on. But he was too far away to see anything much.

Everyone at Sports Day was having fun except him and it didn't seem at all fair that he was left out.

Spot made up his mind and wriggled through the hole again. This time, he'd keep out of sight. He'd find a quiet hiding place where he could watch the races without being seen.

He crept cautiously across the field, keeping a sharp lookout. Some of the smallest children in the school were having a sack race, and they were all getting tangled up in their sacks and falling over. Everyone was watching the race so no one noticed Spot at all.

On the grass was a pile of sacks that weren't being used. Spot crawled towards them on his tummy and quickly burrowed his way underneath them.

He lay still for a moment or two, then carefully poked his head out and looked around. He soon dived back under the sacks again, though, because the first thing he saw was Mr Brown's shoes. The headmaster was standing right next to him!

"Class 3M! Skipping race next!" shouted Mr Brown loudly.

Spot knew that Matt was in Class 3M, so he risked a quick look out from under the sacks again. Luckily Mr Brown had walked over to the starting-line.

Spot had quite a good view, and he was thrilled to see Matt and Daniel lining up next to each other with

176

skipping ropes. He longed to bark loudly to encourage Matt, but he didn't dare.

"On your marks!" Mr Brown boomed, as the entrants stood holding their skipping ropes ready. Spot could hardly sit still because he was so excited.

"Get set!"

It was then that Spot noticed little

Emma Parsons, Daniel's sister, in the distance. She was toddling along on her own across the field, stopping now and then to pick a daisy.

Spot could see that Emma's mum was talking to Mrs Robinson. She'd probably put Emma down for a minute and not noticed that she'd wandered off, Spot decided.

Then Spot noticed something else: Emma was heading towards the open gateway at the top of the field.

Spot knew that beyond the gate was a very busy and dangerous road. Out on his lead with Matt, Spot had seen all sorts of huge scary lorries and buses on that road. Fast cars raced along it too. Spot was sure that little Emma shouldn't go near the road on her own.

"*Go!*" shouted Mr Brown.

At the same moment Spot leapt to his feet and rushed out from under the pile of sacks. He had to stop Emma from going through the gate. But would he make it in time?

Chapter Five

Spot took the quickest route towards Emma – which was straight across the track.

"It's that pest of a dog again!" roared Mr Brown furiously as Spot suddenly appeared and dashed in front of the skipping children. All of them, including Matt, had to stop quickly, and most of them tripped on their skipping ropes and fell.

"Spot!" yelled Matt, trying to untangle himself from his rope. "Spot, come here!"

Spot took no notice. He knew he was a fast runner, but this was the fastest he had ever run in his life.

"Matthew Robinson! Will you get that dog of yours under control!" Mr Brown was shouting at the top of his voice as he dashed down the track. "I've had just about enough of this!"

"I'm trying, sir!" gasped Matt, who was still trying to untangle himself.

"I want that dog caught and taken

away immediately— *Aaargh!*" Mr Brown tripped over a trailing skipping rope and fell flat on his face.

"Are you all right, Mr Brown?" asked Mrs Robinson, who had hurried out from the audience to help.

"Yes, yes, never mind me!" Mr Brown muttered furiously as he struggled to his feet. "Just catch that dog!"

"Spot!" shouted Mrs Robinson. "Come back, right now!"

Spot ignored all the noise behind him and kept going, his eyes fixed firmly on Emma. Suddenly the field seemed very big and very long – and every second was taking Emma closer to the open gate and dangerous road beyond it. Spot wasn't sure he could get there in time, but he knew he had to try.

"Spot!" Matt was racing along behind him, followed by Mrs Robinson, Mr Brown and some of the other teachers who had joined in the chase. "Spot, will you *please* come back?"

Just then, Daniel Parsons noticed

something. "Look, Mum!" he shouted. "Isn't that Emma heading towards the gate?"

"Oh my goodness, so it is!" gasped Mrs Parsons, her face turning pale. "She must have wandered off!" Mrs Parsons and Daniel leapt up and ran after the others.

Mr Brown had noticed Emma too and had forgotten about being angry with Spot. "Quick!" he shouted. "That child is heading towards the open gate. She'll be out on the main road any minute!"

"But look, Spot's trying to stop her!" Matt shouted in an excited voice. "Go on, Spot! Good boy! You can do it, I know you can!"

Spot heard Matt's shout from behind him and forced himself to run even faster. His legs were so tired, but Emma was almost at the open gate. Spot knew he had to make an extra big effort now to reach the toddler and somehow stop her going through it.

Yes! Spot leapt past Emma and swerved to a stop in front of her, making her stop too. By now they were right next to the gate. The sound of lorries and cars racing along outside was deafening.

"Dog!" said Emma happily, having

no idea she had been in such danger. She patted the puppy. "Spot!"

Spot barked weakly. He felt as if he had no breath left. He'd just run the most important race of his life – and he'd won!

Chapter Six

"Good boy, Spot!" Matt reached Spot and Emma first. He picked his puppy up and hugged him.

Mrs Parsons was right behind Matt. She grabbed Emma and gave her a big hug too. "You shouldn't have gone off like that, Emma!" she said tearfully. "But thanks to Spot, you're safe!"

"Spot's a hero!" Daniel added as they walked back to the race track. All the children and parents and teachers cheered the puppy.

Only Mr Brown stayed silent. "Er . . . well," he muttered, as everyone turned to look at him. "I think that er . . . Spot . . . has done very well. Very well indeed . . . And he's welcome to stay and watch the rest of Sports Day . . ."

Everyone cheered and pretended not to hear when Mr Brown added, ". . . if he promises to behave himself!"

Spot barked loudly with delight, wagging his tail. He even thought about leaning over to lick Mr Brown's hand, but he decided against it. Spot still found the headmaster a bit scary!

Everyone sat down, ready to continue with Sports Day. Mrs Parsons kept a tight hold of Emma's hand.

Mr Brown announced that they would hold Class 3M's skipping race again, so Matt had to hurry off.

"I'm really proud of you, Spot!" he whispered in Spot's ear before he handed the puppy over to Mrs Robinson. "You showed Mr Brown just what a brilliant dog you are!"

Spot's heart swelled with pride. He sat on Mrs Robinson's knee to watch the skipping race, hoping that Matt would win.

Sadly, Matt and Daniel got tangled up in each other's ropes and they both came in last. Spot was a bit disappointed but this time he didn't try to interfere and stayed quietly on Mrs Robinson's lap.

It was great fun watching all the different races, and Spot barked loudly through all of them, even the ones Matt wasn't in.

The running race came last, and Spot thought that Matt had a good chance of winning. He sat forward eagerly as children from Class 3M lined up at the top of the track.

Matt waved at him. "I'm going to try to run as fast as you, Spot!" he called.

Spot barked his support then turned round and licked Mrs Robinson's chin excitedly.

Mr Brown got ready to start the race. "On your marks! Get set! *Go!*" he shouted.

Matt and the others started running. Spot was dismayed to see that at first a tall girl with very long legs was in the lead, but then he saw that Matt was catching up with her.

"Go on, Matt!" he barked. "You can do it!"

Matt heard Spot barking and that made him run even faster. He passed the girl and crossed the finishing-line – first!

Mrs Robinson was almost as excited as Spot, and she jumped up and down with the puppy in her arms. "He won, Spot! He won!"

Spot was so proud he couldn't stop barking. He had been hoping and hoping that Matt would come first in a race, and now he had!

When the last race was over, it was time for Mr Brown to present certificates

to the winners. Their names were called out one by one, and each winner went up onto the platform to shake hands with the headmaster.

Spot waited impatiently for Matt's turn. When Matt went up on that platform, Spot was going to bark louder than he'd ever barked in his life!

"And now the Class 3M running race," Mr Brown announced. Spot's tail began to wag furiously. "Our winner is . . . Matthew Robinson!"

Everyone clapped as Matt went up onto the platform, but they laughed too, because Spot was barking madly.

Mr Brown gave Matt his certificate,

then he turned to the audience. "Sports Day is almost over now, but I have one very special presentation to make before we all go home."

Everyone sat up, wondering what was about to happen.

"We have a very clever dog here today," Mr Brown went on. "And after a few . . . er . . . hiccups . . . he has helped to make our Sports Day a great success!" The headmaster went a bit red, then laughed along with everyone else. "So it gives me great pleasure to present a special certificate to Spot Robinson!"

Spot could hardly believe his ears. *He* was going to get a certificate?

"Come here, Spot!" Matt called excitedly. "Come and get your certificate!"

Spot didn't need telling twice. He dived off Mrs Robinson's knee and raced up onto the platform.

Mr Brown bent down and patted Spot, then he gave the certificate to Matt.

"Look, Spot!" Matt knelt down and showed him the certificate.

"It says:

For Spot,
the bravest and fastest dog we know.
From all the children and teachers
at Redhill Primary School."

Everyone cheered and clapped. Spot was so pleased and proud he couldn't even bark. This time he *did* jump up and lick Mr Brown's hand!

Mr Brown smiled and looked quite pleased.

"We'll pin it up in the kitchen, near your basket," Matt said as he gave his puppy a hug. "This really has been *Spot's* Day!"

Lily
the Lost Puppy

For Isabel, Peter and Jessie

Chapter One

"Lily! Watch out!" Jack was dragging an empty suitcase across his bedroom floor, right over where Lily was sniffing a really interesting patch of bare floorboard. It was full of new smells because the carpet had been taken up only the day before.

Hmm, thought Lily, as her small

black nose snuffled along the floor. *Just the faintest whiff of mouse. And something else – old biscuit crumbs, maybe?*

"Lily, move!" Jack called out again.

"OK, OK! Keep your hair on!" Lily yapped crossly as she skipped out of the way. Wherever she was, Lily seemed to be in the wrong place at the moment.

During the last few days, the whole family seemed to have gone mad! There were boxes all over the house and everyone was making a huge fuss about packing things into them. Even Jack had been behaving oddly – he'd hardly played with her for ages. And he was supposed to be her best mate!

Lily lay down with her head between her paws. Why was everyone packing their things away? Was it some sort of game? No, it couldn't be, because when she'd started playing in all that lovely newspaper lying on the hall floor yesterday, she'd got into trouble.

Jack packed the last of his clothes into a suitcase and tried to shut the lid. He'd put far too many things in it. Lily watched as Jack bounced up and down

on the suitcase, trying to get the two edges to meet. After a lot of hard work, he managed to get the lid closed at last and clicked the two clasps together.

"*Now* can we play?" yapped Lily, sitting up and cocking her head to one side.

"OK, Lil, we'll go and play in a minute," Jack replied. "I've just got one more thing to do first."

Lily slumped back down again, then spotted a shoelace hanging out of the suitcase. She trotted over and sniffed it. *Brilliant!* she thought. *I'd know that shoelace anywhere. It belongs to one of the trainers Jack uses for football.* She grabbed the shoelace and started tugging.

"Hey, stop it, Lil!" cried Jack.

But Lily carried on. She tugged and tugged, and suddenly the lid of the suitcase burst open. Lily yipped in delight. This was more like it! She picked up the trainer in her teeth and shook it playfully.

"Drop it, Lily!" said Jack sternly. "That's one of my best trainers."

"No way," growled Lily. "It's one of your smelliest."

Jack made a grab for the trainer, but Lily held on, and won. She raced out of the bedroom and downstairs, with the trainer still clamped firmly in her mouth. Jack clattered down after her.

As they raced along the hall, Mr Harper, Jack's father, came out of the living room. "I hope you've finished your packing, Jack," he called. "The removals men will be here any minute."

Lily skidded across the kitchen floor and made for the dog flap in the back door. But the square hole of the dog flap wasn't wide enough for Lily *and* Jack's trainer. Lily bounced back and landed in a heap.

"Aha! Gotcha!" cried Jack, as he caught up with Lily and grabbed the trainer away from her. She then shot through the dog flap and into the back

garden. Jack opened the door and raced
after her.

They followed their usual marathon
route across the small lawn: round the
fishpond – twice both ways, round the
birch tree, across to the vegetable patch
and back down the other side . . . Then
Lily stopped in her tracks as she heard

a deep rumbling sound outside in the street.

"That's the lorry coming to take everything away!" cried Jack.

"What?" yelped Lily. She cocked her head at Jack. "Why would they want to do that?"

"Come on, Lil, we're moving to a new house," Jack explained. "It's got a huge garden. We'll have a great time there!"

Lily went cold all over. Her stumpy little tail went right down, in protest. "But I don't want to go!" she growled. "I like it here!"

Jack took no notice and raced back to the house. Lily followed, feeling very upset. She didn't want to move to a strange new house. She had friends round here. There was Bruce the Labrador at Number 10. And Wendy the Sheltie, who lived round the corner. They met every day in the park. Lily hadn't even said goodbye to them!

The house was now full of men in overalls, clumping all over the place. They were shouting to each other in loud voices and carrying all the furniture out of the house. Mrs Harper, Jack's mum, was fussing round, telling them to be careful.

Lily peered out of the front door and watched the men putting furniture into the huge lorry which was waiting outside in the road with its back doors open. It was all too much for Lily. She started shivering in fright.

Jack noticed and held out his arms. "Here, Lil!" he called. She leapt gratefully into his arms and snuggled against his chest.

"Exciting, isn't it?" said Jack, ruffling the wiry white fur at Lily's neck.

Lily watched as the kitchen table was carried through the front door. "*I* don't think so!" she whined back. "I think it's *scary*!"

Chapter Two

When all the rolled-up carpets and furniture had gone, the men started to carry boxes outside to the lorry. Mr Harper came out of the kitchen with Lily's basket. "Perhaps Lily should come with me," he told Jack's mum. "There's more room in my car for her basket." He started taking it outside.

211

"Hey! Where are you going with that?" barked Lily.

"Don't worry, Lily, all your toys are in there!" said Mr Harper, smiling as he walked towards the front door. "Come on then!" he called to her, over his shoulder.

Jack put Lily down. "Go with Dad, Lil," he said. "I'm just going to say goodbye to my bedroom."

Lily hesitated – she'd much rather stay with Jack – then trotted outside after Mr Harper. He put her basket on the back seat of his large car which was parked in front of Mrs Harper's smaller red one, then nodded towards the open car door. "In you go then, Lily," he said.

Lily jumped in reluctantly and Mr Harper slammed the door shut. Lily circled round in her basket a few times, nudging the blanket around to get her bed how she liked it. Just then, there was a loud crunch as one of the men hit something hard against the lorry door.

"Hey! Careful with that!" Mr Harper called out, and went over to see if anything had been damaged.

Lily whined unhappily. She hated being on her own, and everything was suddenly so strange and frightening. She wanted to be with Jack.

Then Lily noticed that one of the front

doors of the car wasn't quite shut. She leapt out of her basket, over into the front seat and slipped out through the gap.

Back in the house, Jack was nowhere to be seen. *Maybe he's still in his bedroom,* Lily thought. She trotted upstairs, her claws clicking on the bare wooden floorboards. But there was no sign of him.

Lily hung around, having a few final sniffs in the corners of the room before continuing her search.

Then suddenly, something terrible happened. Jack's bedroom door slammed shut. Someone had shut Lily in!

Lily was so surprised she didn't do

anything at first. She heard someone
shutting the other bedroom doors, and
the heavy front door slammed shut.
Then the roaring engine of the lorry
started up. She couldn't believe it.
Surely they weren't going without her?

Lily rushed over and scratched
furiously at the bottom of the bedroom

door, but it was shut tight. She leapt up at the door handle and caught at it with her paw, but the door stayed shut. She began to bark and bark like mad, but the lorry was making so much noise outside, nobody could hear her.

Lily heard Mr Harper's car engine start up. She ran over to the window. But even when she stood up on her hind legs, she was too short to reach the windowsill.

"See you there!" she heard Mr Harper shout out as the lorry doors clanged shut.

"OK!" Mrs Harper shouted back. Lily heard his car slowly driving away.

Very faintly, over the noise of the lorry, Jack's voice came floating up to Lily. "Lily did go with Dad, didn't she?"

Lily's ears pricked up. "No, I didn't!" she barked. "I'm here!" She scrabbled a bit more under the windowsill, trying desperately to reach it.

"Yes, I saw her get in the car," Lily heard Jack's mum reply. "She'll be there, waiting for you at the new house."

Lily's heart pounded with fear and panic, thumping painfully against her chest. "No!" she barked. "Don't go without me!"

"Hey!" she heard Jack say. "That sounded a bit like Lily!"

"It can't be," his mum replied. "She's gone with Dad. I told you – I saw her get in the car."

Lily took a deep breath and leapt as high as she could, above the windowsill, hoping that Jack would see her. But she couldn't stay up in the air, and he didn't look up at the right time.

Lily's brown pointed ears twitched as she listened to the doors of Mrs Harper's red car slamming shut. The engine started up and the car pulled slowly away, following the rumbling removals lorry. Lily heard it make the crunching noise it always made when it was going round corners. It must be

turning into the avenue where she and
Jack walked to the park.

The sound of the engine slowly faded
away, then disappeared completely.
Lily was alone.

Lily stayed at the window for a while,
listening for the sound of the car to
return. Surely they would come back

for her? But the street remained silent. She began to whimper. Her white furry body quivered with shock.

Then, suddenly, a little spark of courage lit up inside her. "Come on! Be brave!" she told herself.

She stood up and shook herself, then circled the room trying to think what to do next.

She looked at the door. Maybe, if she tried really hard, she could jump up high enough to reach the door handle with her paw. Then she could get out of the house, run down the street and catch up with Jack.

Yes!

Lily went over and started to leap up at the door handle. At first she kept missing. But she kept on, jumping again and again on her short, strong legs. At last, she caught the handle with her front paws. It jerked down as Lily fell back, and the catch gave way. The door swung open. She'd done it!

Lily pushed the door further open with her nose. In a flash, she was out of the room and streaking down the stairs. She skidded across the bare floorboards of the hallway towards the kitchen and . . .

. . . slammed straight into the closed kitchen door. For the second time that day, Lily landed in a heap. The door was shut tight, and the handle was much higher than the one in Jack's bedroom.

Lily would never be able to reach it. All was lost!

She slumped miserably against the door and let out a howl of despair.

Then Lily heard the sound of a car engine outside. Doors slammed. She heard voices and footsteps coming up the front path. Jack had missed her, after all, and had come back for her.

Hurrah!

Lily ran to the front door, her little stump of a tail wagging so hard she thought it would fall off.

She heard the rattle of keys. "Woof!"

she barked happily. "I'm still here!"

"What was that?" said a woman's voice.

"What does Mrs Harper mean?" wondered Lily. "Surely she knows it's me!"

The keys rattled a bit more, then the front door swung open. But the people standing in the doorway weren't Lily's family.

Chapter Three

"Goodness!" said the lady who wasn't Mrs Harper. "What are *you* doing here?"

Lily's heart sank as she looked up at the strangers. "What are *you* doing here?" she barked. "I wanted it to be Jack!" Lily's mind raced. She didn't want to stay here! There was only one thing to do.

Lily shot out of the front door past the strange family, down the path and out of the gate. She ran down the street, heading in the direction in which she'd heard Mrs Harper's red car going.

"Hey! Where are you going?" barked Bruce through the gate at Number 10.

"Sorry, can't stop!" woofed Lily breathlessly over her shoulder. "I've got to find Jack!"

Lily raced round the corner into the road lined with trees. She knew it like the back of her paw – it led to the big noisy road at the end, with the park on the other side, where she and Jack went for walks. Without even stopping to sniff at lamp-posts she ran on, with the wind rushing past her ears.

At the corner Lily skidded to a halt. How would she know which way the red car had turned next? She growled in despair, looking up and down the road.

In the doorway of the corner shop she spotted Yeoman, the old sheepdog who lived there. *He might have seen which way the car went,* thought Lily. She trotted eagerly up to him.

"What are you doing out on your own, Lily?" he asked.

"Something terrible has happened," she whined. "My family have gone to live somewhere else and left me behind by mistake!"

"Oh dear," Yeoman replied. "Don't you think you'd better go back and wait for them? They're bound to come back for you."

"*No!*" yelped Lily. "Some strange people have arrived at the house!" She asked Yeoman if he'd seen Mrs Harper's red car, but he hadn't.

"But Wendy might have seen the car," Yeoman suggested. "She sees everything in this street! She's just gone off to the park with her owner."

"I'd better go and find her," Lily said. She trotted briskly to the main road.

A loud motorbike sped past, making Lily jump. Her brown eyes opened wide with fright. She cowered on the pavement for a while. The traffic seemed even noisier and faster than usual. She'd never tried to cross a road on her own before. If only she was here with Jack, and on her lead.

Then Lily noticed the black and white stripes on the road, where she and Jack usually crossed. The traffic had stopped there and people were walking across, so Lily followed, lost amongst a sea of legs.

As soon as she reached the other side, Lily darted through the park gates. She looked round, searching for Wendy, but there was no sign of her.

Lily trotted over to the pond, where she and Jack used to have such fun feeding the ducks. Her tail drooped sadly. "Oh, where *is* he?" she howled.

At that moment, Jack was slumped miserably on the stairs at the new house. "I *did* hear Lily barking in the old house!" he wailed at his parents. "And now she's run off and I might never see her again!" His shoulders heaved with sobs.

The Harpers had arrived at the new house and discovered the terrible mistake. Mr Harper had thought Lily was still in his car when he'd driven off. After all, he hadn't seen her get out. But when Mrs Harper phoned the old house, the new family had told her they'd seen Lily – and she'd run off!

"We must go and look for her, straight away!" Jack cried.

"OK," his mum agreed. "Let's go. Dad can stay here and start the unpacking."

Back in the park, Lily sat by the pond, her small body shivering, despite the sunshine.

"Hey! What's the matter?"

Lily looked up. It was Wendy, the Sheltie, coming towards her, wagging her long feathery tail. Wendy's owner was sitting on a bench nearby.

"What are you doing out here on your own?" Wendy asked.

Lily told her the whole sad story and asked if Wendy had seen Jack go past in his mum's red car.

Wendy put her head on one side and thought hard. "Well," she began slowly, "there are quite a lot of red cars around . . . but wait a minute!" She yelped excitedly. "Yes, I do remember! It turned into the main road, and went – that way!" Wendy turned her head to point out the direction. "But I'd take the short cut through the park, if I were you," she advised wisely. "Better than going back onto that busy main road."

"Thanks, Wendy!" said Lily gratefully and ran off in the direction Wendy had pointed.

Lily ran and ran, coming to a side of the park that she and Jack had never been to. She slowed down and looked around, panting.

It was all very different here. The shops outside the railings seemed smarter, and the houses and gardens were bigger.

Lily was very thirsty. She found a small puddle and drank greedily from it. *Yuk!* It tasted horrible. She spat it out again.

"These dogs from the other side of

the park have such dreadful manners!"

Lily turned round and saw two large, snooty-looking dogs with lots of silky hair that fell around them like curtains. They were pulling their owner along on two long stretchy leads. They came towards Lily and began sniffing her in a most unfriendly way. Lily noticed they had very smart collars on.

"Oh dear, what kind of scruffy pup is this?" said one.

"And what kind of owner lets such a youngster run loose in the park?" sniffed the other. "Honestly! Some humans!"

The two tall dogs towered over Lily, looking down their long thin noses at her.

Lily's legs stiffened and the wiry hair on her back bristled angrily. They were being rude about Jack! She was about to tell the snooty dogs just what she thought of them when a familiar noise made Lily prick up her ears. It was the crunching sound of Mrs Harper's car engine.

"Excuse me!" she barked, and ran out from behind the two dogs – just in time to see Jack's mum's red car driving past.

Lily yelped with excitement and dashed out through the park gates after the car. She raced down the pavement, dodging people's legs. She just had to catch up with it! Without looking, she galloped out onto the road – then heard a roaring sound, getting louder and louder – and nearer. Lily looked up and saw a big red bus coming towards her!

Chapter Four

Lily cowered, frozen in terror. Then she realised that the bus had slowed down. Luckily for Lily it was stopping to let passengers on and off.

Lily crept back onto the pavement and watched as the bus slowly pulled away again. There was no sign of the red car now. She whined miserably.

Suddenly a strange rumbling noise came from Lily's tummy. She realised she was very hungry! *I might as well go and find something to eat,* she thought.

With a heavy heart, Lily got up and trotted off down the street, sniffing the air for smells of food.

A couple of streets away, Jack and his mum had stopped the car to talk to a lady who was being dragged along by the two snooty dogs who'd been rude to Lily.

"Have you seen a Jack Russell puppy who looks lost?" Jack asked.

The lady thought for a moment, then

smiled. "Yes," she replied. "Not long ago, in the park. Perdita and Polly went up to her, then she ran out through the park gates."

"It must have been Lily!" cried Jack excitedly.

"Did you see which direction she went?" Mrs Harper asked.

The lady shook her head.

Jack's shoulders drooped. "She could have gone anywhere!" he said miserably.

Jack's mum thanked the lady and turned to comfort him. "We'll just keep on looking," she said. "Lily can't be very far away!"

Lily wandered further and further in her search for food. She didn't recognise this street at all. She passed a house with a delicious smell of cooking coming from it and pushed her nose through the gate.

"Rarrghhh! Rarrrghhh!"

Lily leapt backwards in fright as a huge pair of snarling jaws appeared from nowhere. They belonged to an enormous black dog who loomed above her in a very scary way.

"Scram, pup! This is my patch!" he snapped.

Lily didn't hang about. She turned

tail, running and running, until she came to an alleyway lined with dustbins and big black bags. Food!

She started nosing around the bags. When she found one that smelled promising, she tore it open with her sharp white teeth.

Inside, she found a stale crust of bread and the remains of a hamburger, which she gulped down hungrily.

"You can tell this one hasn't been on the streets for long!"

Lily turned to see a pair of scruffy mongrels staring at her. They looked a bit rough, but they were wagging their tails in a friendly way.

"Oh, pardon me," woofed Lily politely. "Is this your patch?"

The two mongrels wagged their tails harder. "We don't believe in that sort of thing," said one. "We strays range far and wide! We hunt in groups and share everything."

"So what's your story, little one?" asked the other stray. "Have you been away from home long?"

Lily poured out the whole sorry story. The two mongrels listened, cocking their heads sympathetically.

"Don't worry," said one of them, when she'd finished. "You're not alone any more. My name's Sam and this is Shep. We'll look after you. Come with us and we'll find you a delicious meal!"

Lily followed her two new friends through a maze of narrow side streets and alleyways until they came to a courtyard full of dustbins. They smelled strongly of all sorts of delicious food.

"Here we are!" announced Sam proudly. "The back of Marcello's restaurant. Best nosh in town!"

In no time, Sam and Shep had raided the dustbins and brought out a variety of tasty leftovers. There was steak and chicken, with crunchy biscuits for afters. They all tucked in greedily.

"Well!" woofed Sam, when they'd all had their fill. "I think it's time to visit the dump and see if we can find anything interesting to chew on. It's a great way to round off a good meal! Coming, Lily?"

"Well, I'd like to," replied Lily politely, "but I really must keep on looking for Jack."

The other two dogs looked disappointed. "Aren't you going to join our gang?" asked Shep.

"If you don't mind, I'd rather not," said Lily. "But I'm very grateful to you both. I'll never forget your kindness."

Sam cocked his head at her. "It's

a great life on the streets, you know. Freedom, independence, adventure . . ."

"But I want to be with Jack," Lily explained. "He means more to me than anything in the world."

Lily trotted on until she came to a neighbourhood on the edge of town with wide, tree-lined roads. The houses were bigger than the one she had lived in with Jack. They had bigger gardens too. Lily could see fields and woods in the distance. But she was exhausted and sat down to rest.

"Oh, look at that little puppy. She must be lost!"

Lily looked up and saw a girl about the same age as Jack, with her parents.

The girl came towards Lily and held her hand out. "Come here, puppy," she coaxed.

Lily shrank away at first but she was too tired to run any more, and these people looked very kind and nice. They reminded Lily of her own family. She let her tail give a tiny wag.

"What shall we do with her?" said the girl's mother. She picked Lily up and inspected her collar. "There's no name tag or telephone number," she said.

"Can we keep her?" asked the girl excitedly.

247

"No, Sally," said her father. "She must belong to someone. We'd better take her to the Dogs' Home. They'll look after her till her owners come and get her."

Lily found herself being carried into the driveway of a nearby house and placed on Sally's lap in the back seat of a big yellow car.

Sally began to stroke Lily, slow soothing strokes along her furry head and back. Lily began to feel sleepy. She gave Sally's hand a lick then curled up, ready to have a snooze.

The car engine started up. Then suddenly, as the car pulled out of the driveway, Lily heard a familiar sound. It was the crunching noise of Mrs Harper's car engine, coming round the corner.

Lily's ears pricked and she sat up, wide awake again. She jumped off Sally's lap and stood up on her hind legs to peer out of the back window.

There were Jack and his mum in the red car! Jack's face was streaming with tears. They were pulling into the driveway next door!

Lily started to bark, but Jack couldn't hear her. The yellow car was gathering speed now, taking her further and further away. She whined, then started

to howl at the top of her voice.

"It's all right, puppy," said Sally, stroking Lily again. "Calm down. You needn't be frightened of the car."

"I'm not!" Lily barked back. "You don't understand! I've finally found Jack and now you're taking me away from him!"

Chapter Five

The blanket in Lily's cage at the Dogs' Home smelled funny, like the stuff Jack's mum used to clean the kitchen. Lily circled round on the blanket a few times, then settled down. She was in a large, bright room full of other cages.

Lily had never seen so many dogs in her life. There were all sorts of colours, shapes and sizes, barking and whining in different voices. They had all looked up when she'd been brought in, then carried on making their din.

Lily's heart felt sad and heavy. What if Jack didn't come to find her? She'd never see him again! She sighed and settled down into a fretful sleep.

"Oh, Mrs Boyd, why did you have to leave me on my own!" whined a voice very close by.

Lily opened one eye and peered into the cage next to her. The spaniel sitting there looked very sad. "Hello, I'm Lily," she woofed.

"I'm Charlie," the spaniel replied.

"Who's Mrs Boyd?" Lily asked.

"She was my owner," whimpered Charlie. "We were very happy. But then she was taken to hospital and never came back. Her neighbour brought me here."

Lily's heart went out to Charlie. He was even worse off than her! At least Lily could hope that Jack would come and get her. "Perhaps someone will come along to give you a new home," said Lily kindly.

"No they won't," replied Charlie sadly. "People only want puppies. I'm two years old!"

Lily decided to try and cheer Charlie

up. She started telling him all about her big adventure on the streets, and all the dogs she had met, until his sad, brown eyes began to close in sleep . . .

By morning, the two dogs were firm friends, snuggled up on each side of the cage wall that separated them, fast asleep.

"Here she is! Lily, did you say her name was?"

At the sound of her name, Lily woke with a start and looked up. She blinked and looked again. She couldn't believe her eyes! There, in front of her cage, was Jack! With Mrs Harper, and Sally, the girl who'd brought her here yesterday!

"Lily!" cried Jack. "I'm here! I've come to get you!"

Lily yelped with delight and sat up, wagging her tail so hard it became a blur.

A girl in a green uniform opened the cage and Lily leapt into Jack's arms, licking his face all over. She wriggled so much he nearly dropped her.

Jack was crying and laughing all at the same time, and Mrs Harper looked a bit tearful too.

"There, Jack! I told you we'd find her!" she said in a rather wobbly voice, dabbing at her eyes with a tissue.

"What an amazing coincidence, Lil!" said Jack. "Somehow you found our new street yesterday. And when Sally and her family came round to welcome us, they told us they'd just taken a lost puppy to the Dogs' Home. It was you!"

Lily licked one of Jack's ears happily. "Yes," she woofed. "Amazing."

"Come on then, Lil! Let's go and show

you our new home," said Jack, putting her lead on.

Lily suddenly remembered Charlie. She looked over Jack's shoulder to say goodbye to him.

"Bye, Charlie!" she barked. "Don't give up hope!"

But Charlie was busy wagging his tail and snuffling away at Sally, who had crouched down beside his cage and was talking to him in a soppy voice.

Once Lily had seen her basket in the kitchen of the new house, the idea of living there didn't seem so strange after all. Jack loved his new bedroom, and Sally had come round to play in their big new garden. She and her family lived next door.

Early one morning, a few days later, Lily was stopped in her tracks as she raced around the garden. She'd heard yapping in Sally's garden. It sounded familiar.

She ran up to a hole in the fence and peered through. Her small black nose touched another, bigger, black nose. Lily recognised it instantly.

"Charlie!" Lily yelped in surprise. "What are you doing in Sally's garden?"

"It's my garden too, now," Charlie woofed happily. "Thanks to you,

I've found a new home!"

Charlie explained that when Sally had arrived back from visiting the Dogs' Home, she'd told her mum all about the spaniel she'd made friends with. She'd persuaded her parents to go and see Charlie. They'd liked him too and had brought him home with them.

"That's great!" yipped Lily happily. "Now *I've* got a friend next door, too!"

"Charlie, come on, let's ask Mum if we can go next door and play with Jack and Lily," said Sally's voice from the other side of the fence.

"See you in a minute," barked Charlie. He turned and ran over to his new owner, his long silky ears flapping.

Lily gave a little leap of joy then trotted off to find Jack. She was bursting with happiness.

Jack came running out to meet her. "Come on, Lil, race you to the rockery!"

"Wait a minute!" barked Lily, her tail wagging hard. "Our friends are coming round. We can all race together!"

Coming soon!

Coming soon!

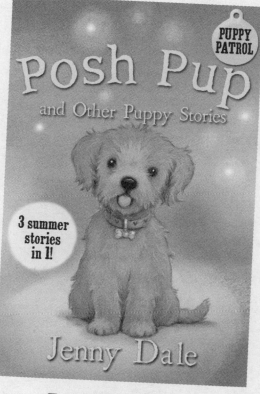

For older readers